Frances Cross wrote a number
of books for teenagers. Sadly,
Frances died in April 2007, and
Marty's Diary is her last novel. It
is also considered to be her best.

Marty's Diary

FRANCES CROSS

SADDLEBACK
EDUCATIONAL PUBLISHING

CUTTING EDGE

Breaking Dawn
DONNA SHELTON

The Finer Points of Becoming Machine
EMILY ANDREWS

Marty's Diary
FRANCES CROSS

The Only Brother
CAIAS WARD

The Questions Within
TERESA SCHAEFFER

Seeing Red
PETER LANCETT

© Ransom Publishing Ltd. 2008
This edition is published by arrangement with Ransom Publishing Ltd.

SADDLEBACK
EDUCATIONAL PUBLISHING
www.sdlback.com

ISBN-13: 978-1-61651-762-5
ISBN-10: 1-61651-762-X

Printed in Guangzhou, China
0512/CA21200795

16 15 14 13 12   2 3 4 5 6 7

I was fortunate enough to be able to work with Frances Cross on Marty's Diary. *We only ever communicated via e-mail, but in the brief time that we worked together, we did become friends and her warmth and professionalism are qualities that I came to cherish.*

God bless you, Frances.

Peter Lancett
Series Editor

Marty's Diary

June 12th
My dad remarried yesterday. He married Linda Fleming. She says she's pleased to have gained not just a husband, but a daughter too. But I know she's lying. She never talks to me if she can help it.

And she's always hanging around and never giving me and Dad time on our own. Linda's never been married before and she doesn't seem to have many friends except for her younger sister, Paula, who lives in Waco. She's always writing letters. How Jane Austen is that? Nobody writes letters in this day and age. She's even had letterhead printed. *From The Desk of Linda Richmond.* I think she's been presumptuous. I mean, she arranged that before they were even married.

They got married at the courthouse on Ridgeway Street and it was a pathetic ceremony. Not like the photos of Mom and Dad at their wedding. This time there was nobody extra except us and Auntie Wedgie, my dad's sister, and Uncle Bill, her husband. She's not really named Wedgie, but everybody calls her that. Auntie Wedgie is okay. I don't think she likes Linda either.

Just before we went off to the courthouse, Linda asked me if I wanted to borrow some of her eyeshadow. She's always trying to pretend we're best friends, but I said no. I don't want to borrow her germy eyeshadow, and besides it was a horrible color.

When Mom got married she had pink roses, and there were some pink roses in the courthouse yesterday. My throat felt prickly when I saw them because I thought of Mom. But anyway, Mom probably wouldn't care because she's happy living in Mexico with her new husband, Juan. They've got a baby now and he's nearly six months old. It seems funny to have a little brother who's a baby. His name's Xavier. But I'm cool about Mom being there.

Then we went to have a reception at the Happy Duck. Linda raised her eyebrows when Dad gave me a taste of his champagne because she said 16 was too young to be drinking. Honestly, I think she lives in the dark ages sometimes. The reception was okay I suppose, but Linda shouldn't think me and her are going to be best friends or anything. Dad looked a bit stupid if you ask me, the way he was touching Linda all the time.

June 20th

I was doing my homework today for Miss Hammond when Linda came in and asked me what it was about. It's really boring and I don't think she would understand it, so I said I could manage. Then she said she would do my colors with Color Me Beautiful. I want to find out if I am a winter or spring or whatever, but I said no. I bet Linda's a spring. My mom's a summer for sure. She always wears pale blue and pink and such, and she looks great. Linda's not bad-looking, but she wears really old-fashioned stuff sometimes. That fits in with her letter-writing thing, I suppose.

From The Desk of Linda Richmond

June 22nd

Dear Paula,

Well, we've taken the plunge and tied the knot. It was very low key which is what Kevin wanted, but Marty was a bit sullen. She's quite polite, but I get the sense she doesn't like me a lot. I've taken your advice and am trying to make friends with her, but she makes it hard. Sometimes I look at her watching me and she almost seems to hate me. I knew it would be difficult to be a stepmother, but I didn't realize it would be this hard.

And Kevin makes such a fuss over her, you'd think she was two years old. I suppose she is his little princess and has a special place in his heart, but it always seems as if he puts her needs first.

All the best,

Linda

From The Desk of Linda Richmond

June 24th

Dear Paula,

There's been an e-mail from Kevin's ex in Mexico. She wants Marty to go and visit her later in the year. I think it's a good idea, but I know if I make too much noise about it they'll think I want to get rid of her. That sounds a bit childish, doesn't it? But a bit of me would find it easier if she wasn't around. Kevin doesn't seem to understand I want some time with him alone as well. Anyway, we'll just keep on going and see what happens.

All the best,

Linda

From The Desk of Linda Richmond

June 28th

Dear Paula,

I am really struggling with this girl. I suspect that beneath the sullen attitude there is probably quite a nice girl trying to get out, but at the moment she's so far under the surface it's impossible to reach her. I tried everything, even offering her a chance to do Color Me Beautiful with me to see what her colors were, but she turns me down flat each time. It's a bit discouraging.

Actually, I think I'm also over-sensitive. Between you and me, I sometimes feel quite embarrassed about behaving like such a child. She's supposed to be the teenager not me, but she winds me up so much. And I do resent the way Kevin treats her as if she's a fragile piece of china. Everything that she wants and needs comes first. I think the problem is that I'm not really used to kids anyway, especially rebellious teenagers. I'll just have to keep on trying my best, but I really wish I had a bit more quality time with my new husband without Marty sulking around the place all the time. Some honeymoon eh?

All the best,

Linda

June 30th

Mom sent an e-mail to ask again if I can go out there and visit them in Mexico. Wow! That's cool. I'd really like to go. Mom's broke so she can't pay. I'd have to get the fare from Dad. I want to see an Mayan pyramid. Plus my friend Becky says that Mexico City, which is where Mom lives, is great. Mom went there on vacation two years ago and said the sun shone all the time. So after she and Dad split up, she went to live out there. I don't think Dad and Linda will mind me going to see her. I think they'll be glad to get rid of me, especially Linda. To be honest, I don't think Dad will even notice if I am here or not. He spends all his time with my darling stepmother these days. When I asked him if he wanted to go skating like we usually do on Thursdays, he said that Linda wanted to do something else. So I went by myself. It was okay. Jazz was there. I'm not interested in him or anything, but he's pretty hot.

Marty's Diary

July 10th

My birthday. I'm a Cancer. I read my horoscope. It said, "someone has come into your life who will have a profound effect on it for good or ill." That means Linda of course. Then it said, "keep all your options open." I don't know what that bit means unless it's something to do with going to Mexico at Christmas. Anyway these horoscopes are crap. If they'd said "a tall, handsome man (Jazz) has come into your life" I might believe them. Everybody at school thinks he's great. I told him about Linda. He said stepmoms were okay and he's got one so he should know. But I think it's different for guys. I looked up Linda's horoscope—she's Sagittarius. It says she needs to relax more and go with the flow and let the universe show her what it has to offer. Huh.

Also I got a great present from Mom—a really cool top and a CD I wanted. Guess what Linda and Dad gave me? Well, it was a really ugly dress thing with flowers on it. Linda said it was the right color for me. Honestly. Which planet is she on?

July 16th

I'm in my room. Dad sent me there for mouthing off to Linda. I think he's ridiculous the way he reacts. It's her fault for treating me as if I were 10 years old. My own mom doesn't do that. I hate her. Dad's being really unfair. I wish I was in Mexico with Mom. She wouldn't treat me like dirt. If I was a bit older I'd go by myself.

July 30th

I had an e-mail from Mom this morning. She said that if Dad can afford it, she'll ask if I can go over there in November. It will be warm there. I hope I can. I really want to see Mom again and get away from horrible Lumpy Linda.

August 1st

That's it! I have finally had it! Dad says I can't go to Mexico until I "adopt a better attitude." He's even starting to talk like Linda now. He's going to see how I do in September with my schoolwork before he'll decide if I can go on vacation. It's all stupid anyway. And now it's the holidays and I'm stuck at home with HER.

The only good thing is that Jazz is still around and he's going to take me to this new place which is a club he knows about. I'm not telling Dad about it and will sneak out when he's canoodling with Linda.

August 2nd

Dad says I can't go out again for three weeks. He's just making a ridiculous fuss because I missed my curfew and I had had a drink. It isn't like I'm an alcoholic or anything. And he said Linda had said she smelled cigarette smoke in the bedroom. Dad said she didn't want to narc on me or anything, she just felt worried that I might be getting addicted to smoking. Huh. She just wants to make trouble, that's all.

And another thing. I am sure it's only Linda that's stopping Dad from buying me a plane ticket to Mexico. I bet she's said it would be a waste of money and he shouldn't do it.

From The Desk of Linda Richmond

August 15th

Dear Paula,

How are things? It's a bit grim at this end. I had to tell Kevin about Marty smoking in the bedroom and I have to admit he did come down on her a bit hard, but I was doing it for her own good. If she gets hooked now she might never be able to stop. Kevin's really worried about her at the moment because her schoolwork is really going downhill. I think he's starting to feel a bit guilty about her actually. He seems to think my coming on the scene is causing all her problems. It's making things a bit difficult between us and I'm treading on eggshells.

Because she's not behaving well Kevin's said that he's not prepared to shell out for her airfare to Mexico until she shows she is making an effort. The trouble is that I think Marty believes I'm responsible for his decision. If she only knew! I would be really

pleased to get her long face out of the house for a bit!

Anyway, when Kevin calms down a bit at the beginning of next semester I'll see if I can persuade him to let her go to Mexico. It can't do any harm, and she might come back in a better frame of mind. It sounds ridiculous but a bit of me is beginning to wonder if I have made a mistake going into this marriage in the first place. I love Kev, there's no doubt about that, but I didn't count on the difficulties of coping with this girl. And it doesn't seem to get any easier either.

All the best,

Linda

August 22nd

I am so fed up. She is so, like, in my face the whole time. She's a neat freak and if I leave anything lying around she gives me grief about it. It's stupid. I've asked Dad if I can go and stay with Auntie Wedgie for the weekend. She's got a new dog and I could help her exercise it and all that. Auntie Wedgie didn't mean to get the dog at all, but she couldn't resist it when she saw it at the pound where it needed a new home. She said nobody else wanted the dog because it was too big.

August 24th

Am staying with Auntie Wedgie who is the most messy woman in the universe. She asked me how I was getting along with Linda. So I made a face and said not very well. "You'd better try," she said, "because she's with your dad now." I could see she was struggling to find something nice to say about Linda. In the end she said, "She's got nice hair."

I like the new dog. He's called Spotty and he's a mutt with long floppy ears. He is the worst-behaved dog I've ever seen. He chews on everything, but he's got a nice nature.

August 28th

Back home and am hanging out with another friend of mine called Ben. He's cool about stepmoms and reckons I am not really being fair to Linda. That's 'cause he's really nice about everyone though. Anyway, I don't care about anything. I'm just going to have a good time. I'm sick of schoolwork and everybody nagging me about grades. It's not like I want to go to college or anything. Dad would like me to go because he says I am very bright, but I think it's because he wants to brag about having a daughter in college.

Maxi Lorne is having a party tonight. It'll be great. I'm going even though Dad would freak if he knew about it. They can't keep treating me like a baby. I can catch up with the English assignment next week.

Marty's Diary

August 30th

Because I had such a bad report from school, Dad says I definitely can't have a ticket to Mexico. I told him that that creep Paul Stanton, the English teacher, had lowered my grade but he didn't believe me. That teacher's had it in for me since the beginning. He's always lowering my grade. I don't care anyway because I'm having a blast with my friends. Screw the work.

October 22nd

This semester seems to be going on forever. Dad keeps talking about having a nice family Christmas with him and Linda. Huh. I don't know what planet he thinks he's on. As far as I am concerned the best Christmas ever would be on a desert island a million miles away from my precious stepmom.

She's trying to bribe me with presents now, and keeps saying things like "why don't we go down to the boutique on Main Street?"—I'd sooner pull out my own fingernails.

Auntie Wedgie came and took me to Dallas for the weekend which was nice of her. She didn't say anything about Linda, but I can tell she doesn't like her either. She asked me lots of questions about what things were like at home now. I told her how different it was now that it wasn't just me and Dad. I said that Linda was obsessively neat and kept cleaning everything 60 million times over, and that she stressed about even little bit of mess. Auntie Wedgie said maybe I could be a bit neater, but I said that I wasn't that bad. Auntie Wedgie just pointed to the towels on the bathroom floor of the hotel and we both laughed.

We went out shopping and it was great. She's not like Linda, in your face all the time, and pushing clothes at you that would look good on a seven-year-old. Auntie Wedgie just stands back and lets you choose what you want. We went and had lasagna at Luigi's. Auntie Wedgie said casually, "Marty, what's this I hear about your homework? According to your dad, if you go on like this you'll be the bottom of the class—minus, minus grade!" She laughed and I laughed, because she's got a nice way of saying things like that; a way that doesn't make you feel bad. "It's not that bad," I told her, "I've just got a bit behind." She smiled at me. Then she said, "You need to work, Marty. If you get really behind, you'll find it hard to catch up." She looked a bit sad when she said that, and then I realized she was talking about herself. Auntie Wedgie has always said she didn't work at school and she ended up with no qualifications and no job. I think she does mind really, because she'd like to have had an interesting job, not just helping Mr. Patel at the convenience store. Anyway, I promised her I'd work a bit harder. I was actually looking forward to telling my dad the good news—that he had a reformed daughter!

Walked into the house full of good intentions. There was nobody around downstairs although it was after six. I yelled for Dad and eventually he came down the stairs looking a bit harassed. He had a red hot water bottle in his hand. "Hi, Marty," he said, a bit absent-mindedly. "Hi," I said, and I began to try to explain about how I'd decided to work a bit harder at school, but he didn't seem to be listening. He ran his fingers through his hair and said, "That's great, honey," before I'd even finished telling him properly. "I've got to fill this bottle for Linda. She's not feeling too good." He went off into the kitchen. Honestly, I was furious. That stupid woman just has a little stomach ache and then everything in the universe stops for her. "What about me!" I felt like shouting to him, "I'm here too. Don't I matter?" But I don't think he would even have heard me because he was so wrapped up in her. She's probably just got the flu or something. Well that's that! If my own dad can't be bothered to listen to me when I'm trying to tell him something important, what's the point? And it's no use him getting Auntie Wedgie to do his dirty work and try to make me get better grades. From now on, I'm going to do what I want to do! And it will serve him right if I fail all my exams this year. Anyway, I don't care because school sucks.

October 30th
Linda's still hanging around the house with a mopey face. She's making the most of this flu. She gets on my nerves and so does Dad because he's always fussing around her.

Mr. Warren (my math teacher) asked to see Dad this week. He was livid when he came back. He said that creep Warren told him I wasn't making any effort. He told Dad that I was a bright girl, but I wasn't using any of my ability and he thought it was a waste. Naturally Dad went ape and he's on my case all the time now: "Did you do your homework, Marty?," "You're not going out until you've finished that project." Nag. Nag. Nag. When I get to be a mom, I'm not going to treat my kids like this.

I had a letter from Mom today with photos of her and Juan and baby Xavier. He looks cute, but it feels a bit funny to see Mom holding a baby like that. She looks really happy and so does Juan, and I suppose they're a real family now. I'm glad for her, really I am. It's just weird to see her in a family without me and Dad.

From The Desk of Linda Richmond

November 3rd

Dear Paula,

Sorry I haven't written for a bit, but I haven't been feeling too good. Nothing I can put my finger on. Kev says I am just getting stressed and maybe I am a bit. A lot of the problems are about Marty, of course. She's getting worse and worse, and I'm not sure that Kevin's sister isn't putting her up to some of it. I am honestly getting fed up with Marty's whining. If she doesn't get 100 percent of her father's attention all the time, she acts up.

The other thing is that I broached the issue of another child with Kevin the other day. I would really like to have one of my own, but Kevin says he doesn't want another one. He says it wouldn't be fair to Marty and don't I think that we've got enough on our plate trying to meld this family together without adding any more members to it. Maybe he's got a point.

Anyway I am going to take things a bit easy for a week or two. Marie has invited me to stay at her cottage and Kevin thinks it would be a good idea for me to get away for a bit. I'll only stay about a week. I'm going tomorrow.

All the best,

Linda

November 10th

Hurray! Linda's gone away and it's just me and Dad. Things are like they used to be, and he doesn't complain all the time about the mess, and we just eat things like pizza in front of the TV. I bet he likes chilling out a bit as well although he won't admit it. Linda's so, like, old-fashioned. She always wants to eat at a table with a cloth on it and all that. And she doesn't like what she calls junk food, so we all have to eat vegetables and stuff all the time. And Dad's been talking a lot more to me.

He's not so stressed when Linda's away and he just chats about things and doesn't get on my case all the time. I wish it could be like this always. I suppose Lumpy Linda will be back soon though. She can stay away for a year as far as I am concerned.

We talked a bit about Mexico and Mom. I wonder if he ever regrets that they split up. He seemed quite sad about it really. I don't think Linda is the right person for him—she's too prim and proper. He needs somebody like Mom who's a bit crazy. I got the feeling when he talked that he envies Juan a bit, although he would never admit it. Anyway, he said that if I did work a bit harder he would see whether he could manage the airfare in the New Year so I can go and visit. "What do you think about having a new brother?" he asked me. I told him I was totally cool with that and looking forward to seeing the baby. I think he was surprised because he expected me to be jealous.

November 20th
Dad and me are still on our own—Yay!—although Linda is coming back tomorrow. Anyway, he said we can go to the mall this afternoon and do some shopping.

We had a great day and got a little furry toy to send to Xavier. And then Dad said we can't forget it is Linda's birthday next week and we should buy her a present. He asked me what I thought she would like, but I couldn't think of anything, so he went and got her a gold bracelet. It was really beautiful. I said he never bought things like that for Mom, and he said that was only because he couldn't afford them in those days. But it spoiled the day really because he didn't even get me anything. He tried to make up for it by saying he'd buy me something special for my birthday as well, but that's easy to say. My birthday isn't for ages.

From The Desk of Linda Richmond

November 26th

Dear Paula,

Well, I'm back home again. I feel a little bit more relaxed so hopefully things might get easier, although we didn't start off too well. Kevin bought me a beautiful gold bracelet for my birthday and I love it. But old nose-out-of-joint Marty just looked really upset about it. Why shouldn't he buy me something? I am his wife after all. Listen to me—I feel a bit ashamed that I am complaining about a teenager like this. I sound like a teenager myself. But she does wind me up so much. Mind you, what you said was right—I need to try to forget it isn't just the stepmom/ stepdaughter thing but the fact that she is a teenager. My friend Mellie Symes says it will be a miracle if her teenaged daughter makes it to twenty-one, she's driving her so nuts.

We're going to Wedgie's this evening. I do find that woman quite hard to read. She definitely seems to resent me a bit as well.

All the best,

Linda

November 27th

Went to Auntie Wedgie's for dinner yesterday. It was okay and she'd made some really nice things to eat, but Linda said she couldn't eat some of it because she has a problem with green peppers. Auntie Wedgie seemed a bit tense, and she wasn't as chatty as usual. I think she's worrying about Jamie. My stupid cousin is a few years older than me, and he's never worked since he left school. He lives with losers and doesn't wash and he's a creep. Also he's got a bad temper and is really bossy with me, like I'm his baby sister or something. It bugs me. I know that Auntie Wedgie is worried about him, as if she hasn't got enough to put up with, with Uncle Bob. She told me about two years ago all about Bob, and how he's unfaithful. She said she doesn't care any more, but I think it makes her unhappy. Bob never says much at all, just sits and stares into his beer.

Anyway something happened at dinner because Linda asked Auntie Wedgie about her job. To be fair to her I think she was just being polite, but Auntie Wedgie went very red in the face and was quite rude to Linda.

I think she feels embarrassed that she just works in a convenience store. Linda went to college, something she doesn't let us forget, although it doesn't seem to have done her much good. She ended up working in an insurance office before she married Dad. I think one reason she married him was to get away from that.

Went back to Auntie Wedgie's to take back a DVD I'd borrowed. She was sitting at the kitchen table, just staring at nothing. "Uh-oh," I thought, "it's that Bob again." But when I spoke to her she didn't move and didn't throw china around the way she usually does when she finds out about Bob's antics.

So I put the kettle on and made her some herbal tea, and gave her a cookie because I read somewhere that's what you do for people in shock, and she looked as if she had had a shock. She still hadn't said anything and I was getting worried. "Drink your tea," I said.

"I've lost my job, Marty," she said then, and burst into tears. I know Auntie Wedgie's job isn't perfect. Old Mr. Patel is really cheap, but it is a job and they're few and far between around here. And she's been there forever, about five years I think. "Why is he firing you?" I asked her. She said he wasn't firing her, just closing down the store altogether. "I can't blame him," she said, "he's not making much money at all now, what with the new Walmart opening down the road."

Well anyway, I stayed with her until she'd finished her tea and she looked a bit better after that, although she was really upset. And I don't know how they will manage because Bob doesn't earn much either, and there's Jamie as well. Auntie Wedgie's always worried about him what with having no job and living on unemployment with those creepy roommates. The only member of that family who's okay is Spotty. He's grown into a huge dog and Uncle Bob complains about him all the time. I like him. I take him for walks sometimes, which nobody else does. He pulls a bit so it's more like a run than anything else.

I told Dad about Auntie Wedgie when I got home. He just gave me a hug and told me he thought she'd get another job soon. Then Linda went and spoiled everything again when she said, "I wouldn't have thought that was a great job anyway. Surely Wedgie can find something a bit better than that." I really hate her sometimes. She's seriously insensitive.

From The Desk of Linda Richmond

November 29th

Hi Paula,

We went and had a really ghastly dinner at Wedgie's house a couple of nights ago. She seemed in a peculiar mood and that husband of hers never opened his mouth. The next day Marty went there and heard that Wedgie had lost her job. So that was why she was so sullen. I really think people need to help themselves a bit more. Surely she could have gone to college. These people make their beds and have to lie in them the same as the rest of us. Anyway, Marty is busy being Florence Nightingale and going off to see Wedgie every five minutes. It keeps them both happy I suppose.

I'm still feeling ill, but better than I was. It's clear to me now that Kevin's not going to change his mind about my having a baby. And I suppose it would be risky at my age anyway. But I really feel bad about it because I would so much have liked to have

had children. Kevin says that as Marty and I get a bit closer things will improve. But at the moment I don't see that happening in my lifetime with the way things are.

The Mexico trip is still on and off and so we have Marty in our hair for the foreseeable future. She still isn't knuckling down to work at school. Her father keeps trying to talk her into working harder, and I have a gentle word now and again, but it just goes in one ear and out the other. I felt like saying to her the other day that if she didn't pull her boots up she'd end up like Wedgie with no qualifications at all and a dim future ahead of her. Of course I didn't because it would have been cruel. So we struggle on, and the more we push her the more obstructive she becomes.

All the best,

Linda

December 3rd

Just been raked over the coals by the principal, that creep Halitosis Humbert. Nobody ever sees him because he hides in his office most of the time except in emergencies. A lot of the teachers have been complaining about me so he called me in.

"Your attitude is totally unacceptable, Marty Richmond," he said. "All I hear from your teachers is that you are rude and that you don't do any work. Oh, yes, and Mrs. Hammond says you are a bad influence on some of the other girls." I just stared at him. He's horrible that man, with his bad breath and his hair combed across his bald patch. Nobody in the school thinks anything of him, and now he is lecturing me. "You have had numerous warnings," he said, "and if I don't see a considerable improvement in your behavior we may have no choice but to consider expulsion." I stared at him. The others sass teachers too, and they don't get hassled. Why is he piling it all up on me? Well I don't give a crap about him—there's no way I'm letting him get to me. I told Jazz about it and he said maybe I should try a bit more at school because expulsion's no joke. Huh. Some friend. You'd think he would support me a bit more.

December 5th
HUGE CRISIS! I went to see Auntie Wedgie on my way to school because she's under a lot of stress just now, what with losing her job. I found her sitting in the middle of all the mess in the kitchen just crying and crying. Well I couldn't leave her, could I? And Spotty was being really delinquent as well. He'd got hold of the telephone book and was shredding it all over the floor. So I stayed for an hour or so and made her coffee and cleaned up and said I'd come back later. And when I got to school the teacher screamed at me! She didn't even give me a chance to explain anything. She just marched me down to the principal's office. He didn't give me a chance either. He just sent me home. He said I have been suspended for a week while they decide what to do with me. They phoned home to tell Dad what had happened, but of course he wasn't there and Soppy Linda took the message.

I could almost see her cheering inside to think that Marty is in trouble again. She was all pale and washed-out looking and she said she couldn't deal with the stress of this. Then she clutched her heart. Honestly, what a drama queen. I didn't even bother to explain anything to her. It was a waste of time. I just went into my bedroom and slammed the door shut.

Have just had this major fight with my dad. When he came home he was really angry. He doesn't lose his temper much, but when he does it's like a volcano erupting. He said that I was an ungrateful spoiled brat and if I didn't get my act together very soon, people would start giving up on me. That got to me— so I tried to explain exactly what happened that morning. But he didn't really seem to be listening. He was more concerned about going back to Soppy Linda because she said she was feeling ill with the worry of it all.

I hate him. And I hate her. And I wish I never had to go back to that stupid school.

At least I thought I would get some support from Auntie Wedgie. After all, it was because of her I was late to school in the first place, but when I told her what had happened she didn't even seem to take it in. Huh. That's what happens when you try to help people.

And worst of all, I have been grounded now and Dad says I can't go out with my friends for a week. Not that I could have done much anyway because he hasn't given me any money for ages. And now he's come up with the worst idea yet. He wants me to work at his office on Saturdays. He's asked his boss and they have agreed to hire me. It will be so like totally boring. I can't believe it, and they are paying me next to nothing. It's slave labor really.

December 8th
I've just been hanging out in my room for days now. I'm bored out of my mind and it will even be a relief to go and do this job at Dad's office tomorrow.

December 10th

It's okay at Dad's office, actually. They've given me really boring things to do, like making the coffee and stuffing envelopes, but it beats being at home I guess. And I get a chance to spend lunchtime with Dad. They've got a staff cafeteria, and everybody goes there. Dad seems more relaxed when he's at work which is weird. You'd think he'd be more relaxed on his time off. Everybody seems to know him and he's really popular. One of the people I met was Cassie Shaw, who used to be his girlfriend before he took up with Linda. I think he might have married her if Linda hadn't appeared on the scene. Cassie's nice although she's really young. We had a bitching session about my beloved stepmom because she hates her as well.

Anyway, when we were on our own I asked Dad again about going to visit Mom. He wasn't so negative this time. I guess he just wants to get rid of me!! But he did ask me what I thought about the baby. I said, "Little Xavier? I'm fine about him. It'll be great to have a little brother. I can boss him around when he's bigger." But Dad didn't laugh. He just said that I should remember that things between me and Mom might not be the same, now she's got a new family and a baby. I told him I wasn't dumb and knew that. But I reckon he's exaggerating. Me and Mom have always got along. She wanted to take me with her when she left, but she didn't have a job or anything so it wasn't possible. That's why I got to stay with my dad. Besides, I love my dad a lot. I wouldn't want to be separated from him.

Yeah, these Saturdays have been great. He's told me a lot about his life when he was younger. He never did that before. He told me about the trip to Corpus Christi they made every year without fail, and how his dad used to sit on a deckchair and read the newspaper while his mom did her knitting. My nana was great at knitting, but she chose horrible colors for things. I reckon she got the yarn cheap somewhere. It was always gray or navy, except for one orange sweater she made me. I had to pretend it had been stolen because I was too embarrassed to go out in it. Anyway, Dad said they didn't have much money but it was an okay life.

So it looks as though I might be able to go out to Mexico after all. Mind you, there is a condition. I've got to do better in my tests at the end of the semester. So I'm trying a bit now.

From The Desk of Linda Richmond

December 10th

Dear Paula,

How are things there? It's been a bit more peaceful here because Kevin has got Marty a job in his firm on Saturdays. The rest of the time she does seem to be knuckling down a bit more on her schoolwork as well. But her attitude is still ambivalent toward me. I put up with so much and then I lay down the law. Well you have to, don't you?

All the best,

Linda

From The Desk of Linda Richmond

December 11th

Dear Paula,

I've just had the most tremendous fight with Kev. It all came up because of the redecorating and revamping of the house, including recarpeting. He's been promising that we can do it all after Christmas and I've been really looking forward to it. I'd organized everything and the decorators were starting on January 7th. And then today he says we'll have to put the plans on hold for a few months! When I asked why, he got quite irritable and said that he didn't have a bottomless pit of money whatever anybody thought. But I said, "We've agreed to do this, Kevin." Then he said a man was entitled to change his mind and that he'd decided to use the money for something else. I couldn't believe it! He is actually abandoning our decorating plans just so that spoiled brat can go to Mexico! I pointed out that the house was looking so shabby I was almost ashamed to be asking people

over. Then he got really nasty and said he didn't realize he'd married a Beverly Hills housewife. So now things are really tense between us. I said that he was being unfair, and he said, "My daughter must come first." Well, now we know. I feel like getting out and leaving them both to it.

I'm getting so fed up. I can't even imagine how horrible Christmas is going to be. Kevin thinks we should spend it with Wedgie and Bob and I don't suppose that'll be a bunch of laughs. Wedgie just sits there staring into space. I think I preferred her when she never stopped talking.

All the best,,

Linda

December 22nd

My test scores were crap. Dad is furious and Linda is going around with a smug sort of I-told-you-so face on. But still. I don't care because I'm going to Mexico! Yay! It's confirmed at last. And guess what? Dad isn't even paying for the ticket, Juan is. Mom sent an e-mail to say Juan thought it was high time he met his stepdaughter and the ticket was his treat to me. What a guy! I can't wait. Linda is really sour about it, although I can't think why because she just wants to get rid of me all the time. I don't think Dad's that pleased either. But he can't refuse to let me go if somebody else is paying. Just think—in another three weeks I'll be in Mexico City with Mom and my new family! Wheeeeeeeeeeee! Mind you, we had to get special permission from school for me to be away. And they've given me tons of work to do while I'm over there, even though I'm only going for three weeks.

PS: I've still got Christmas to get through. We are going to have turkey with Wedgie and Bob and I'm not looking forward to that I can tell you. Linda will sit there and look at Auntie Wedgie as if she's a bad smell under her nose. And Dad will make bad jokes to try and show everybody that he's enjoying himself.

December 24th
Christmas Eve. I've been thinking about Jesus. I mean who said he was born on December 25th anyway? It could have been another time for all we know. I reckon Jesus was an okay guy. He had the right ideas anyway. And I guess he wouldn't have been horrible to anyone. Maybe there's a message there. Maybe I have to try to be nicer to my dear stepmom. Hmmm.

Forget it. I'm not going to be nicer to somebody who is so in my face all the time. She made me help her get some food ready to take to Auntie Wedgie's. Normally Auntie Wedgie buys a turkey from Kroger and burns it in the oven. But Linda says that these things should be done properly. She wants home-made stuffing and cranberry relish and gravy. So she's told Wedgie she'll cook it all and we'll take it there, like Meals on Wheels.

December 26th

I thought Christmas Day would be terrible, but it wasn't too bad as it goes. I have to say the food was really great. Linda may be a pain, but she can cook when she puts her mind to it. I think Auntie Wedgie was a bit peeved, but she did her best to be nice. Anyway we ate until we were stuffed, and then had some of Linda's pecan pies which were really light and crumbly. Mind you, it was all really forced, with everybody wearing stupid paper hats and playing party games. I don't know why anybody does that. They never do it the rest of the year, and everybody looked really dumb. Uncle Bob was wearing a pink hat with a gold band on it and looked ridiculous.

It's freezing cold today. I went for a walk because I was fed up being inside, and all my friends are away for the holidays. I went past the haunted house on the hill and found myself outside St. Stephen's Church.

It's a nice old church. I went inside and saw the crib with baby Jesus lying asleep and Mary and Joseph—who looked a bit like Regis Philbin—leaning over him. I always think that baby Jesus looks cold in those cribs without any clothes on. I wished I'd had a blanket to cover him up with. That made me think of Xavier. I wonder what he's like. I've seen pics of course. But I can't really imagine him. Not long until I'm in the sunshine of Mexico. I can't wait! Bert at the garage says the sky in Mexico is bluer than you can imagine. Mom says it's warmer there than here so I must take clothes with me that I can layer.

January 11th

I'm on my way to Mexico at last! This plane is a bit more like a sardine can than an airplane with so many people squashed in it. But I don't care. I'm so excited. The woman next to me asked where I was going and I said Mexico City. I can hardly believe it myself! It's going to be great. I can't wait to see Mom and tell her all about Linda and Auntie Wedgie and everything. Mom says sometimes we're more like friends than mom and daughter and I know what she means. She says we can go shopping together and that's great. Mom knows what to buy when we go out together. It's going to be fabulous!

January 14th

Wow! Mexico is great! The sun shines all the time, so you don't have to worry about getting soaked when you plan a fiesta which is what they call parties here. Everybody is really relaxed. Mom and Juan live in an old Colonial house just below the university in Mexico City. It isn't theirs—they just rent it. But it's really nice. There's a kind of huge enclosed garden with lots of plants and flowers we don't get in Texas. There's a really strong-smelling white plant called *huele de noche*. I think whenever I smell that in the future I'll think of this place. And Xavier is so sweet. Mom seems to have to give him lots of cuddles and he doesn't want to leave her at all. That's fine though. I'm okay with that. Mom looks beautiful—she's put on a bit of weight, but it suits her, and she wears nice linen trousers and shirts. Juan's great, and always has lots of stories to tell. He's really tall, about six foot four, and is a Spaniard. He seems totally cool about my being here. There's no tension. No more now, diary. I must go and make a salad for the fiesta they're having this afternoon.

January 18th
This is such a great place! Imagine waking up every morning to sunshine and you'll know what I mean. I could seriously live here all the time. We can't do all the things we want to do, because Xavier needs quite a bit of attention. I wanted to go shopping with Mom yesterday, but we couldn't go

because Xavier gets bored and cries. But like Mom said, that's fine. We can always go another day.

Juan has had to go away for a few days, so it's just the three of us. Mom says tonight when Xavier's in bed we can pig out on the sofa and eat pizza and tons of totally fattening things.

January 19th

We had pizza but we didn't get a lot of chance to talk. Xavier's teething or something, so he kept waking up and crying. Mom's great, and we did talk a bit but I don't think she was really able to concentrate on anything but the baby. That's okay. We've got loads of days to talk. The main thing is that we are together again. Mom said she was really pleased to see me. She said she missed me a lot. I told her I missed her as well. I wish I could come here and live close to them. I wouldn't get on top of them or anything. Perhaps when I've finished school I can come out here and get a job or something. That would be great.

January 23th
We're all going to dinner in Mexico City this evening. Mom's got a baby sitter and Juan's back home so he's going to treat us. I'm going to have fish because they do great fish here. Yay.

Had a fantastic time at the restaurant and we ate outside. I took lots of photos to show everybody at home. Make Linda jealous as well! It's great eating outside—and Mom and Juan were really nice to me. Juan talks a lot, and he knows a lot about all sorts of things. But he's really kind. Mom gave me a necklace she'd bought me, and they both said I looked good in it. I wish I could live here all the time. Everybody is so relaxed. After the meal we went home to watch *March of the Penguins* on TV which is a film about penguins of course. I thought it was boring, with these penguins standing around in the snow looking freezing cold and miserable. But still.

January 29th

Still enjoying myself. Sent a load of cards to my friends at home. They will be so jealous when they see the pre-Colombian pyramids. Teotihuacán is a huge ancient city. We got to climb the Pyramid of the Sun. The view was amazing. Went to the Alameda Central which are lovely gardens. There are some really beautiful plants there and it's great walking around it. I think Dad would like it a lot. I wonder if he's ever wanted to visit Mexico. I don't think Linda would like it, because she gets freaked out with creepy crawlies, and she wouldn't like the spiders and mosquitos and things. Mom says you get used to them.

Marty's Diary

From The Desk of Linda Richmond

January 30th

Dear Paula,

Hello from a nice and tidy quiet house! Marty's been gone a while and it is so much more peaceful around here. Mind you, such is the irony of these things, I almost find myself missing some things about her. But not the wet towels on the bathroom floor or the dreadfully loud music. Definitely not those.

Judging from the e-mails, she's enjoying herself over there. It helps to have unlimited warm weather I guess.

And in the meantime Kevin and I are doing some of the things we had to put on hold before. Now that Juan has kindly paid the airfare for Marty, there's a bit of money to spare. So Kevin decided we would go ahead and do some of the redecorating, and so that's been great and very therapeutic. I really couldn't stand the wallpaper that Mel had in the den. It was a horrible color, and *clashed with the carpet. We've got a much softer look now. And Kev found a man who can re-do the kitchen for about half the price of the first quote. I think he's Guatemalan or something. In fact, Kevin thinks we should do the whole house while we're at it, including Marty's bedroom. He says it might be a nice surprise for her when she gets back. I just wonder if perhaps we should talk to her about it first, but Kev says it will be fine. She'll just be happy to know we made a bit of an effort for her.*

Kev went to see Wedgie yesterday. He seems to be quite worried about her, and Bob never seems to bother at all. He doesn't seem to notice that Wedgie isn't herself. She isn't even trying to get work any more. And that Jamie is completely out of control. He hasn't been back to visit his mom for weeks. Kevin said that Wedgie seemed almost unworried about him. It's a bit strange. But she did say she was missing Marty. I guess she would be because she and Marty are close.

Well, another peaceful week to go and I'm going to make the most of it. I've invited

a couple of my friends here for a meal this evening. Kevin doesn't know them so it's a chance for him to get to know a bit more about my friends. I went to college with Liza and she's married to a stockbroker. They live in Dallas. Since we don't often entertain, I thought I would push the envelope a bit and do something special. I love cooking. I find it therapeutic.

All the best,

Linda

From The Desk of Linda Richmond

February 3rd

Dear Paula,

Well the Guatemalan man has been and gone and he was fantastic. So neat—not leaving paint smears everywhere. The den looks much better now, and so does the kitchen. Mel has her style and I've got mine, and they are completely different! Mind you, I don't know what young Madam's reaction will be when she gets back. But we took a lot of time choosing the colors for her room. I made rich red curtains and the walls are cream and we bought her some colorful rugs and some posters. It looks suitably teenage and vivid. I think she'll like it.

The dinner party was a success although Kevin was rather quiet. But Luke and Liza made up for it. They were great. Luke asked Kevin about his work and they chatted a bit about that. Kevin doesn't know much about stockbroking so he couldn't say a lot. He's not the only one!

Marty's Diary

I'd better go—I have to run out to the grocery store for a few things. Marty is back in a couple days and the fridge needs restocking.

All the best,

Linda

February 3rd

I can't believe how quickly the time has gone. It seems only five minutes since I arrived here. I am getting used to be being here now, although it would be better if I had more time to spend with Mom on my own. She's always so busy with Xavier. If he's not teething, he's pooing or something. Ugh. That's all babies seem to do. Poo and pee all the time. She's always changing diapers. Yesterday I went through to the bedroom and she'd just changed him, and was cuddling him really close. I wondered if she cuddled me close like that when I was little. Of course I know she did really. Anyway, I asked her, and she called me a big softy and gave me a mammoth hug. Mom's hugs are lovely. She always smells of flowers and talcum powder. Then she asked me if I was okay about having a baby brother. She said, "You don't feel as if you have been pushed out, do you Marty?" Well I said, "No, I didn't." You have to say things like that when somebody asks that sort of question. But I think the truth is I do feel a bit left out. I mean, Xavier's always there, isn't he? Mom tries to get me to be more involved with him. She asks me to change his diaper and bath him, but I am all fingers and thumbs. But anyway, he's a nice little thing really.

I had an e-mail from Jazz today. He said he was missing me. Ha ha. He never really bothers with me much when I'm there. He said it was boring without me to liven things up.

Went with Juan to the art gallery that he runs. It's called Meso-Art and there are paintings and sculptures and things from all over Mexico. He gave me a cool present. It's a figure carved in jacaranda wood of a woman and a child. He said it was made in Chiapas. Juan's a really kind guy.

Helped Mom clear out one of her closets before dinner. She has a maid called Loli who comes in once a week, but she doesn't have time to do much except clean. So Mom was clearing away all sorts of clothes that she said she was going to give to Loli. I remember a lot of them, and it gave me a funny feeling to see her put them on a pile of unwanted things. Still, it's ridiculous to expect her to keep some seriously old-fashioned outfits just to keep me happy. Anyway, I showed Mom the photo I always keep in my wallet of us all from when I was small. Mom looked at it and laughed. She said she had a dork hairdo in those days. Then she gave me back the photo. She said, "You really miss those times, don't you Marty?" So I said I did. And then I think she must have read my mind because she said, "I suppose you wonder why your dad and I broke up?" Well I do wonder that as it happens. So I just nodded. And Mom didn't speak for a moment. It was like she was trying to sort it out in her own mind. Then she said, "We were really young when we got married. I don't think we really knew what we were doing." So I said, "But you did love each other." Mom shrugged and said she did love Dad but that wasn't always enough. They grew apart and that was that. It sounded sad and wrong to me, but there wasn't anything I could say. Mom took hold of my hand. She said, "Marty, I'm with Juan and your dad's with Linda, and we've all moved on. We couldn't go back to the past even if we wanted to."

So now I'm confused. Does Mom regret leaving Dad? I know one thing. I'm never getting married unless I am totally completely certain that he's the right guy.

Must stop now and go and get ready. Juan's taking us to this great restaurant just outside the city. Yum. Must make the most of my time because in two days I'm going to be back in rainy old Texas. One thing though, I'll be glad to get back to my room and have my own things around me again. I guess I am sort of a bit homesick. Even the idea of Linda doesn't seem too terrible. I MUST be homesick!

From The Desk of Linda Richmond

February 10th

Dear Paula,

Well here we are almost snowed in! I wonder what it's like at your end. And things are a bit frosty in the house as well. Marty got back safe and sound from Mexico, but she was absolutely livid about the redecorating. She said it was bad enough that we'd completely changed the den and the kitchen, but she was really, really angry about the changes to her room. She said that was her space and we shouldn't have even have touched it without her permission. I did mention that to Kevin when we decided to do the room, but he thought it would all be okay. In a way I understand why Marty's upset. It was the only link she had with her past. We should have left it. I feel bad about it. I should have been much more sensitive. After all, it was her home before it was mine and I know she still hopes against hope that somehow her mom and dad will get together again, although she knows it's completely ridiculous to even think it.

All the best,

Linda

February 12th

I can't believe what she's gone and done! I got home and found my bedroom completely changed. Everything I like about it was altered. It was a sort of cream color before with all my favorite posters on the walls, and the old rocking chair in one corner. I had my favorite cover on the bed which was one Mom and Dad gave me years ago. It was like a sort of patchwork in green and pink. And now it's all really bright colors and the cushion on the rocking chair has been recovered and I have new curtains. I feel like those people on that old TV show, *Trading Spaces*, who hated it when their rooms had a makeover. No, I feel worse than that. I feel really angry that they have totally changed everything without my permission. They didn't even ask me!!! I AM SO FED UP! BLOODY HELL! And the den and kitchen are different too. In fact it doesn't look anything like our old house at all. It looks like Linda's house. I wish I was back in Mexico. I wish I was anywhere but here.

Marty's Diary

February 14th

Valentine's Day! I had two valentines. I know one was from Auntie Wedgie. She's been sending them since I was little and always tries to disguise her writing. I don't know who sent the other one. Maybe Jazz. Wedgie teased me about both of them, although we both know one of them was hers. I went to see her on the way home from school. She is looking quite ill and has lost weight. It was weird. I went through to her bedroom and she had a few weird things in there. There was a food mixer in a box, some exercise equipment, and some new clothes that didn't look like her style. She said she'd got them in a sale. I'm wondering if she's beginning to lose it. I told her how I hated the new decoration of the house, but she didn't say anything much. She didn't seem to be listening. And the house was quite dirty as well. Spotty had been chewing one of her best shoes and she didn't even seem to notice. I took him for a walk because I think he's bored and acts up because of that. Maybe we should try to get him another home. Bob never bothers with him at all, and even Wedgie doesn't seem to remember if she's fed him or not.

Had a really huge fight with Dad. He said I am ungrateful. He was angry because I yelled about my bedroom. He said, "We plan this wonderful surprise and Linda works her socks off, and all you can do is moan. You need to straighten yourself out, young lady." How would he like it if someone messed with his room? I tried to explain this to him, but he was too irritated to listen. So in the end we just had a huge screaming match. This didn't help anything. I'm fed up with him taking her side all the time. Whatever happened to loyalty to me? All I ever hear from him is loyalty to Linda.

February 20th
I've just been to Auntie Wedgie's. She arrived home at the same time as I arrived. But it was weird—she had a bag over her arm which she tried to hide when she saw

me. "What's that?" I said, "Been shopping again?" Although I thought it would have been strange because she hasn't got much money now that she's lost her job. Anyway she laughed it off, but something wasn't right. I suddenly realized something—I remembered the other things in the room and I said, "You've stolen it." But she shook her head. I followed her through into her room and we had a big fight about it. I'm sure she stole all those weird things she has in the bedroom. She just didn't want to tell me. I don't know what to do about it. To start with, the things she's taken are so weird. I mean why would she want to get home exercise things? She never exercises. When I got back I tried to tell Dad about it, but he didn't really listen. He said he was in a hurry and had no time for my nonsense. But I'm worried. Something's not right.

February 25th
Got yelled at in English again today for not paying attention. But I couldn't help it. My mind was on Auntie Wedgie and the weird stuff in her room. I wish Mom was here. I

could talk to her about it. I can't really write it all down in an e-mail. I am really, really worried about my aunt. She's behaving so strangely these days.

When she was getting dinner, Linda seemed to be less grumpy and wasn't as prickly as usual. And I found myself telling her about Auntie Wedgie. She was quite sympathetic which surprised me. She said she would go and see Wedgie, and she told me not to worry too much. Maybe she had bought all those things for a reason. I don't know that it was a lot of use telling her, but I did feel a bit better about speaking to someone.

Marty's Diary

From The Desk of Linda Richmond

February 27th

Dear Paula,

How are you? Things are plodding along here as usual. Although one unusual incident was the fact that Marty actually consulted me about something. Yes, it's amazing isn't it? Well, apparently she'd gone to Wedgie's house on a previous occasion and seen a pile of new things in Wedgie's bedroom which Wedgie wouldn't normally buy. Then a couple of days ago when Marty went to visit her she bumped into Wedgie arriving back home, clutching a bag that she seemed to be trying to hide. Marty confronted her and asked her if she'd stolen the stuff, but she denied it. But Marty is convinced that her aunt is stealing. Marty's problem is that she can't understand why Wedgie would take such bizarre items. She said, "It didn't feel right."

I am beginning to wonder whether Wedgie is menopausal and losing it a bit. I think I need to talk to Kevin about this and then I'll go and see Wedgie.

All the best,

Linda

From the Desk of Linda Richmond

February 28th

Dear Paula,

I really intended to go and see Wedgie, but when I talked to Kevin about it he said it was ridiculous and that Wedgie would never steal anything from anyone. He said that he thought Marty was exaggerating as usual. I told him that I'd said to Marty that I would go and visit Wedgie, but Kevin put me off. He said it wasn't really our business. I don't know if he's right because I can't help feeling a bit uneasy about it somehow. And the things that Marty found in the bedroom were so unlikely—things like gym equipment and a wok and so on. Not the usual things you would expect Wedgie to buy. I don't know quite what to do. I promised Marty I would go there and I will. But I don't know whether I should confront her about these things or not.

All the best,

Linda

February 29th

Leap year! Yay. Not that it matters to me because there isn't anybody I want to propose marriage to. It's freezing cold and the central heating has died. Dad is wandering around muttering to himself and Linda seems to be all weird. Mom sent a fantastic picture of Mexico City, with the sunset in the background and the clouds turning red. I wish I was back there again.

Went to see Auntie Wedgie this afternoon. Although it was late she hadn't even bothered to get dressed. She was wearing an old bathrobe and just sitting in a chair. It made me sad to see her. She's usually rushing around and it's weird to see her like that. She said Linda came to see her. But Auntie Wedgie didn't know why. She said Linda talked about nothing for about five minutes and then went away. So she never spoke about the things that Auntie Wedgie had in the bedroom. Anyway I made her some coffee, and I tried to make her laugh a bit by telling her about my baby brother and the things he does. She said it did her good to see me, and cheered her up. Spotty was being his usual self and climbing all over the sofa and that. I don't think Wedgie notices him half the time. If you ask me that dog's not all there. But he's got a nice nature just the same.

March 10th
Have been trying to see Auntie Wedgie at least twice a week. But she still seems strange. I asked Linda why she didn't ask Wedgie about the things in the bedroom. She said it was too awkward. That made me feel a bit mad. Something's wrong with my aunt. I know it is. I must speak to Dad about it.

Dad says I am exaggerating. He says I am a drama queen and that there's nothing wrong with Auntie Wedgie. But there is.

March 15th
I knew I was right! Auntie Wedgie was arrested for shoplifting today in Dillard's.

She'd taken totally weird things—two pairs of roller skates and a lemon squeezer. How anybody in their right mind could think she was all there when she took those things beats me. And when Dad went to the police station he said she was just standing there in a daze. She didn't even seem to realize that she'd done it. I knew she was all wrong. If she wasn't married to somebody useless like Uncle Bob maybe somebody would have done something before now. Nobody listens to me, and now look what's happened. Anyway Dad took her home and made her some tea and phoned Bob. I'm going to see her tomorrow on my way back from school. I'll take her some cookies. She likes cookies.

March 16th

Just got back from Auntie Wedgie's. I thought she would be upset, but she hardly seemed to be worried about anything. It was so strange. I told Dad I was going to take her to the doctor. He said I am fussing about nothing, but that I could take her if Auntie Wedgie agreed.

March 19th

I went with Auntie Wedgie to see Dr. Marsh, and she said that Auntie Wedgie was suffering from depression brought on by the menopause. She said that lots of women get depressed during that time. She says she'll give her some antidepressants for a bit, and some hormone treatment. Wedgie said I was a help and she was glad she had someone to count on. I'm glad somebody appreciates me!

From The Desk of Linda Richmond

March 20th

Dear Paula,

Well things have been hectic here as usual. Kevin is busy with one thing or another. Marty has been spending a lot of time with Wedgie. Wedgie was caught shoplifting the other day which explains all those weird items in her bedroom. I feel slightly guilty about that because Marty wanted me to talk to her aunt at the time, and I felt too embarrassed to do anything. I have to hand it to Marty, she has been quite good about all this. She insisted on taking Wedgie to see her doctor because she said (quite rightly) that Bob wouldn't do anything. The doctor says she is menopausal and depressed. So she's prescribed hormones and antidepressants which should stabilize her. Marty is there today keeping her company for a bit.

All the best,

Linda

Marty's Diary

April 1st

April Fool's Day. I can't believe it's ten months since Linda and Dad got married. So much has happened. I was beginning to think my saintly stepmom wasn't so bad, but yesterday she went and messed everything up again. Dad said that for my birthday in July I could have a new iPad. Well you should have seen Linda's face. It was so like sour grapes. She said she hadn't realized that Kevin had so much money to splash out on expensive presents. Then Dad got on his high horse and before I knew where I was, they were both shouting. Anyway I'm getting the iPad, thanks very much, although Dad's said that if my schoolwork starts going downhill again he might have to re-think. And then we had a really big fight! I keep telling him that I want to go to nursing school but he says it's not necessary. He wants me to get a business degree. Huh.

April 12th

I went out with Jazz last night and we were late getting back. Dad was livid. He says if I don't get my act together he'll take my allowance away. Like it would make much difference, the amount he gives me. He said I have to go back to the office on Saturdays for a month. He's arranged a job. This time I'm helping a girl called Thelma. It's Dad's really subtle way of showing me what a happy life people have working in an office. He's hoping I'll really go for it and do this business studies program instead of nursing. Fat chance. Why won't he accept that I want to be a nurse?

Some photos of Mom and Juan and Xavier arrived by e-mail today. Xavier's getting a lot bigger. They all look really happy, beaming out from the photo. I wish I was there. I wish I was part of their family. Everything's so cold here—the weather, the house etc. And there are just problems all the time. Linda walks around the house with a sour face half the time, and Auntie Wedgie still isn't right. I've been going there every day after school but she doesn't seem to be bothered whether I am there or not. And now I think that Bob's got a bit on the side. I can't be bothered with Uncle Bob, but seeing how much Wedgie's let herself go, I don't think you can blame him really. I said I would dye her hair for her. It turned out okay, but it's a bit streaky. She laughed when she saw it and said did I think she looked like she was trying too hard. It was quite a bright red but I think it suits her. Then she got really upset afterwards and said she wished that she'd had a daughter and not a son who never did anything for her.

April 15th
Last night Auntie Wedgie took pills and some gin and nearly killed herself. Uncle Bob found her unconscious on the floor in the bedroom. She's in the hospital now "under observation." I wish I'd done more for her. But Dad said I did a lot and if they'd listened to me a bit more maybe this wouldn't have happened. Poor Auntie Wedgie.

April 16th
They let me go and see her today. She is very thin, but she didn't look as dazed as she has. She says she's very sorry for upsetting

everybody. She didn't mean to do it. Only things were just getting to her. Turns out she knows all about Bob and what he's been up to. But she doesn't seem to care about that. I don't think she's loved him for a long time. Maybe it would be better if they just split up.

April 17th
I went back to see Wedgie this evening. She looked quite a bit brighter and was wearing lipstick. I think she feels embarrassed about the pills and everything. I told her that Linda and Dad were coming to see her later and she just nodded. And then just as I was leaving there was another visitor. It was a surprise because it was Mr. Patel from the convenience store. He said that he was sorry to see she was in the hospital. And then he said that he wanted to offer her a job when she was better! He's shut the corner shop and has bought a dry cleaning business, and Auntie Wedgie can go and work there. He'll give her a trial period and if things work out then she can be the manager. Hurray. Things are looking up at last.

Things are DEFINITELY better—I got a really good grade for my last essay. Dad was pleased with me. He said if I keep doing this it will be great. He's even sounding less negative at the idea of my going to nursing school. He said the way I helped Auntie Wedgie was really good. I think he was proud of me although he didn't actually say that. You should have seen Linda's face though. I think she felt a bit jealous because I was getting all the attention. It's her own fault. She never did anything at all to help Wedgie.

May 4th

I couldn't write in my diary for a few days because something terrible has happened! I feel sick when I think about it. About two days ago Linda and Dad cornered me in the kitchen. I realized something was going on because they looked so serious. "What now?" I thought. "What dreadful things has Marty done this week? No doubt one of the teachers has been on my case again." Anyway they just stood there staring at me. It was weird. It was like neither of them knew how to start the conversation. So we all stood there for a few minutes looking at each other like idiots. Then Dad said, and he sounded really awkward, "Marty, we've got a bit of a surprise for you." It took me a second to figure it out. I must be dumb or something because otherwise I'd have realized. "You're pregnant," I said to Linda. She nodded and then Dad went on about it not making any difference to anything. I said, "I thought you didn't want any more children?" But Linda said it was an accident. Accident my foot. I bet she planned it all from the beginning. I really hate the idea of a pooing, smelly baby in the house. And what's worse is that Linda is going around looking so smug. Ugh. Why is she doing this now? She's got Dad—why can't she be satisfied with that?

May 7th
Linda made me go to Babies-R-Us with her and it was seriously boring. I heard her talking to Dad earlier on and she said she wanted to "involve Marty." I really hate it when she does that. So we went looking at clothes for the baby. She asked if I would

like a brother or a sister and I said it didn't make any difference. Honestly, I don't know what she wants me to say. Anyway, she bought loads of things for this baby. It's going to have more clothes than any baby in the universe at this rate. She kept asking me what sort of clothes she should buy. Like I should know. I asked if it was a boy or a girl, but she doesn't know. She says she can't decide whether to find out or not. But I don't care because I'm not interested in it anyway. It has nothing to do with me. They can keep their precious baby. As soon as I can, I'm going to leave home anyway.

From The Desk of Linda Richmond

May 8th

Dear Paula,

Well we finally plucked up courage to tell Marty about the baby. She's been very quiet about it and it's difficult to tell what she's thinking. But like you said, it's almost impossible to tell what any teenager is thinking half the time. Anyway I took her out with me when I went to buy baby clothes.

The book I've got on step-parenting says you have to involve your stepchildren as much as possible. But it wasn't really a success as she was clearly bored. She asked me if I was going to find out the sex of the baby. I wonder if that will make a difference. I suppose, from her point of view, if I have a girl it will be another daughter and competition for Kevin's affection. Anyway, I haven't decided yet whether we should find out about the sex of the baby beforehand. In some ways it will make it easier to plan things.

Kevin was very angry when he realized I was pregnant. But thankfully he's come to his senses and is as excited as I am. Last time he spoke to Mel he told her as well. She seemed to be really angry about it, and I don't know why. She said we were being irresponsible. It's all right apparently for her to go off and remake her life but the rest of us aren't allowed to. And she had the nerve to say that Marty might feel left out, which wasn't fair. My heavens! If anybody has pushed Marty out of the nest it's her.

All the best,

Linda

May 15th

Honestly! All I ever hear about is this baby. It's due in November and I don't suppose Linda will stop talking about it until then. And now she's got Auntie Wedgie knitting things for her. Wedgie's much better now. She's off the antidepressants and really enjoys working in the dry cleaners. It's a place called Smart Suits and Mr. Patel has made it look really cool. Because Wedgie's the manager she's well paid. She looks tons better and seems to feel really good. She's just as nuts as Linda about this baby though. I thought at least my own aunt would have some sense. But she and Linda keep sitting down talking about redecorating the bedroom and prenatal classes and boring things like that. And Linda keeps being so pseudo-nice to me all the time, it's so annoying. It's like she has seen these books on relationships where they say you have to make an effort with your wayward stepdaughter.

Dad's changed his mind about thinking I should study nursing. He says I have to take business classes. He says with my selfish attitude I would be a rotten nurse. Jeez. I mean I did help Wedgie when everybody else refused to.

Had a long talk with Mom. She was worried about how I would feel about Linda's baby. So I said I didn't care. Which is true. And Mom said that she thought it would all be okay really. I don't know who she's trying to convince. To be honest I thought she was trying to convince herself as much as me. I'll never understand why she left Dad in the first place. I know she and Juan are happy together, but she and Dad were happy too, for years and years and years.

Huge drama again because my school-work isn't going well. Honestly, I wish they'd all get off my case. I'm working. Sometimes. Anyway, Jazz and me went all the way the other day. We were in his house looking after his younger brother who was asleep upstairs. I don't know what all the excitement's about. But Jazz seemed to like it. Just as long as I don't get pregnant as well. Ha ha. That would be a laugh.

June 1st

Summer is finally here! I have been sitting in the back garden trying to get a tan. Had a big scare when the condom broke and had to take the morning after pill. But it's okay. Bad enough having one brat coming along with Linda being pregnant. Can you imagine their faces if I told them I was having a baby as well? Anyway, I don't ever want a baby. They cry all night and if they don't have gas, they're teething or something. Dad says I'm not sympathetic enough to be a nurse.

June 3rd

Dad says he's going to confiscate my allowance permanently because he's totally sick of my behavior. But he can take a running jump with his allowance because I'm going to apply for a permanent, part-time job at Sundays Boutique. It was a lot of fuss about nothing anyway. He and Linda went away, and I had Jazz and a couple of friends over. Somebody broke a beer bottle on the dining room table. There's a bit of a mark, but they can cover it with a tablecloth.

And then Dad said I'd scratched some of his CDs. As if. I wouldn't touch them—all that Elvis Costello and stuff. Anyway, now he and Linda are totally freaked. They say I am ungrateful and messy and they are sick of the way I behave. I would so like to get out of here. Jazz is excited about us getting a place together. I don't know what he's going to use for money. His stocking job at the supermarket pays nearly nothing. I wish I could jump onto a plane and just go off to Mexico. Nobody gets on my case there. And there's no one I can really talk to here, except Jazz. Even Auntie Wedgie seems to have less time for me now. Not that I care.

From The Desk of Linda Richmond

June 4th

Dear Paula,

Marty is getting really rebellious now. I think she feels very threatened by the idea of this baby. I don't know why, because we do make an effort to include her in things. She left a horrible mess in the den the other day after she had a party and damaged my cherished dining table.

One good thing is that Wedgie seems to have snapped out of it. Ever since she got this new job at the dry cleaners she's a different person, and she's genuinely interested in this baby. So we have nice talks together about that.

But getting back to Marty, I'm not sure what to do with her. She doesn't really seem to be coming to terms with things. We'd reached a sort of level of non-aggression before we told her I was pregnant. I think she believes I'm having this baby out of malice.

I wish she could realize that it's a dream of mine to have a child of my own. Kevin and I were talking about it last night and he asked me whether I wanted a boy or a girl. I honestly don't know. I think Kevin would like a son, but a bit of me would love to have a little girl. I can't decide whether we should find out the sex of the child in advance. It's tempting, but it's also wonderful to think of having a surprise at the end!

I can't believe this is happening to me. I've waited so long and suddenly there it is—in a few months I will be a mom. It's a dream come true.

All the best,

Linda

From The Desk of Linda Richmond

June 12th

Dear Paula,

Thanks for your last letter. I think your advice about telling Marty how I feel was a good idea. She certainly seemed less aggressive when I told her how much I wanted this child. I tried to appeal to her better nature. I also told her a bit more about my former life and how difficult it had been after I lost Andy when I was just 23 years old. I explained that he had been in the army and it had been a terrible shock. We'd been planning to get married a month after he was due to come home for his next leave. She puzzles me so much, that girl. Sometimes I think she's quite heartless, and at other times she really surprises me with small acts of kindness. Anyway, it didn't do any harm telling her how I really felt and a bit more about myself. Maybe she doesn't realize that I feel a bit vulnerable sometimes as well. I suppose from her perspective somebody

my age has got it all, and doesn't have any uncertainties and fears about things. If she only knew the truth!

All the best,

Linda

June 16th

I bought Linda something for the baby from the Babies-R-Us store down the road. I wasn't going to, but I felt a bit sorry for her after she told me how much she wanted the baby. She's a real pain, but I didn't realize how much sadness she's had in her life. I still hate the idea of this baby, but at least I thought it would be something to get it a toy. I bought a bear. It's called Custard and it's yellow, so it doesn't matter if it's a boy or a girl. Linda made a lot of fuss when I gave it to her. Like I never do anything for her or something. But anyway, I suppose she was trying to be nice. Jazz asked me the other day if I liked her. I don't know if I do or not. So then he asked me if I would like her if she wasn't my stepmom and I said I didn't know. I suppose she's not too bad. I suppose most people are okay really. But she's too different to me. We like different things.

Marty's Diary

From The Desk of Linda Richmond

June 20th

Dear Paula,

Marty actually bought a present for the baby. I was touched to think that she'd gone all the way to Babies-R-Us specially for that. When I tried to thank her she got very gruff and short with me. She is hopeless at taking thanks or compliments. But at least it's a start. Maybe she's coming round to the idea of the baby at last.

All the best,

Linda

June 28th

I went to the steakhouse with Linda and Dad last night. I should have realized there was something up. Linda never goes to places like that. She prefers Luigi's restaurant on Mallow Street. So I should have known they had an ulterior motive. Dad talked about nothing much for a bit. But I noticed he was fiddling with his fork and that made me think he was nervous. "Uh-oh," I thought, "They are going to tell me something I don't want to hear." And after a lot of hemming and hawing he said that they had decided to find out the sex of the baby. They thought it would be a good thing to do. So I said that was fine because it wasn't anything to do with me. But it made me think about it afterwards. And I suppose it would be okay if it were a boy. But what if it were a girl? I'm the only girl. I don't want to share Dad with another daughter. That would be horrible. Anyway, I'll have to wait and see.

Marty's Diary

July 4th

Just been talking to Jazz. He said because it was Independence Day we had to talk with British accents all day. He's psycho, that boy. He was trying to cheer me up I think. I feel down. The baby IS a girl. I felt a bit sick when Linda told me, but I tried not to show it. I mean it's not the baby's fault or anything. But what happens when it gets bigger? I suppose that Dad won't have any time for me at all then. It's all changing. First of all Mom has Xavier and now Dad's going to have this girl. Where does that leave me?

July 18th

Some FANTASTIC news! Ages ago Jazz persuaded me to do a YouTube audition for a talent show called the X Factor which is on Fox. Jazz has a friend who lets him jam on his guitar at his house and can record things. So we went and recorded a song which Jazz wrote called "Finding Me." I like singing. I'm not bad at it. Anyway that was over three months ago and we never heard anything. And now somebody from the X Factor has phoned me and asked me to come and audition at the studio. This is my chance! Maybe I will be famous!

July 25th

I auditioned in this scruffy place that looked like a huge warehouse. I was really nervous. Auntie Wedgie had given me a good luck rabbit's foot to carry in my pocket. But it was great. They had me sing a few songs and said that Jazz's song, *Finding Me* was the best. So they told me that I could be on the show! Yay! Marty you're going to be a star! Jazz is totally proud of me. He says that we might even be able to start a group together.

From The Desk of Linda Richmond

July 30th

Dear Paula,

Marty is in seventh heaven. Things were a bit tricky after telling her about the baby being a girl, but she's so excited now about getting through the auditions for the X Factor that she doesn't think about anything else. I am glad for her, but think she might be heading for a fall if she thinks stardom will just fall into her lap.

At least my relationship with her is slightly on the mend and that's a relief. It has its ups and downs, but it does seem to have stabilized a bit now. I just wish I knew what she really thinks.

All the best,

Linda

From The Desk of Linda Richmond

August 9th

Dear Paula,

It's boiling hot here and I am feeling quite uncomfortable. I thought about what you'd said about Marty and I tried asking her outright how she felt about everything. I asked her if she felt that we were getting along a bit better now. But she brushed me off as if she didn't want to talk about it and immediately changed the subject. So I'm no further forward.

All the best,

Linda

August 9th

Linda needs to get off my case. What does she expect me to say? To fall into her arms and tell her she is the most wonderful stepmother in the universe? Just because you make somebody cookies occasionally doesn't turn you into ideal stepmom material. And she keeps on spouting all this relationship crap to me. It's all about relationships and their parameters, whatever the hell they are. The truth is that I wouldn't want anybody with my dad except my mom. Why can't she accept the way I feel? I don't want to have to tell her the real truth, but if she keeps on nagging me I might have to. It's horrible having a stepmom. You feel as if you are walking on eggshells all the time. I can't feel relaxed and easy with her the way I do with my mom. It all seems tense. It's not a normal thing. She was a stranger to me before she became my stepmom. She's not my family. Not now. Not ever.

Anyway, I'm not going to get upset about her now because I am too excited about being on the X Factor. I will be at the recording next week. There are six singers and if I win I go through to the next round. It's great. Everybody wants me to win, and Linda even bought me some jeans which are really nice. I can't believe that she chose them. She usually goes for boring pants. Marty—the star of the future! Watch this space, diary!

August 20th

I feel gutted. I didn't get through to the second heat at the X Factor show. There was a girl there with a squeaky voice who seemed to really impress the judges. They were way mean and shouldn't have been so bossy I think. It's a stupid show anyway. They don't let the viewers choose who gets to go to boot camp. Anyway I don't care.

Have just had a really massive fight with Dad. He said that I had been neglecting everything for the show and that it was time "I adopted a more mature attitude to things." At least Linda stood up for me. And that's a first! But Dad just said I was totally selfish and always thinking about myself and nobody else, and that I had to get my act together a bit more. Anyway I'm sick of both of them. If I had the money I'd go back to Mexico in a heartbeat.

August 21st

Linda's been wandering around all day (it's Saturday)—and moaning about feeling ill. She's always got something wrong with her that woman. I swear she's got about a hundred pills in the bathroom cabinet, although she's stopped taking some of them recently because of the baby. Anyway, she's been moaning to anyone who will listen. Even Auntie Wedgie, her new best friend, is getting bored with her. She keeps saying she doesn't feel quite right, whatever that means. My mom never complained about the state of her health all the time. She just laughed and took an aspirin. Why can't Linda be the same? Come to think of it, there are lots of differences between the two of them. Mom fusses a lot less about things.

From The Desk of Linda Richmond

August 21st

Dear Paula,

I don't feel well at all today. I'm not sure exactly what's wrong, but I just don't feel myself. In fact, I haven't felt quite right for a bit. But when I mention it to Kevin he just seems to think I'm making a fuss. And as for Marty—she just gets impatient. She and Kevin have been going at it head to head for days now and I'm getting sick of the arguments. I think that Marty just winds him up for the hell of it a lot of the time. She's quite selfish in that way. I wish I could get away for a few days. The atmosphere in this house isn't good for anyone. Don't worry if you don't hear from me for a week or two. I think I'll just take it easy for a bit.

All the best,

Linda

September 7th

This has been a TERRIBLE day! The worst day of my life!! I can't believe what's happened. It's so awful. It started when we were having breakfast and Linda was mixing some horrible granola stuff on the counter in the kitchen. Then she clutched her chest and fell down on the floor. I thought she was teasing for a minute, although that's not her style. Then I realized there was something wrong. Dad leaped across the kitchen, and he could see she was in a bad way. He told me to call 911. She had sweat on her face and was struggling to breathe. It was awful. I called the paramedics and they came very quickly. But I thought she was going to die. I think Dad did too, because he just sat with her head in his lap and looked really shocked.

The paramedics gave her oxygen and they put her on a stretcher and took her straight to the hospital. Dad went with them in the ambulance. He told me to call Wedgie and one or two other people. I think Auntie Wedgie was really shocked as well.

Dad is back from hospital now. I ordered a pizza for us. He looked really white and said that Linda is quite ill. She had a major heart attack. Dad says she almost died. They are doing tests now to find out whether there is any damage to her heart and if she needs an operation. I feel really bad now because sometimes when I've really hated her, I've wished that something bad would happen to her. And now it has, and I feel terrible. What if she dies? How will I feel then? And what about the baby?

September 12th
Things are still terrible here. Linda is still in the hospital. The doctors say they are very concerned about her. And they are worried about the baby as well. So it seems she might lose the baby. I didn't like the idea of that little girl at all. But now that I know it might not be born at all I feel really sad. I know that Dad and Linda think I'm a hard case, but I'm quite squishy underneath. I think Dad is wondering if Linda might not make it at all. I don't think he's thinking too much about the baby at all. He really does love her.

September 14th

Linda is still ill. Still in the hospital. They are deciding if they should operate. Dad's nearly frantic with worry. I tried to cook dinner tonight but it was a bit of a disaster. It was supposed to be delicious spare ribs but they were all dry and funny. Anyway, I don't think Dad would notice if he was eating cardboard. He just ate without really noticing anything. I wish I could help him. And I wish I didn't feel so guilty about everything. What if I had something to do with her heart attack? What if I hassled her so much that she wasn't able to cope any more. I am trying to pretend that it doesn't worry me, but it does. There have been so many times recently when I've wished she would just disappear off the face of the earth.

I went back to that church again. I never go to church, but I just thought I would. It was very dark in there, and if Jesus was there it was hard to imagine. I tried to think of something to say, a sort of prayer really, but I couldn't find the right words. So in the end

I just said "I'm sorry about everything. Can you make Linda better?" But I felt like an idiot. And there wasn't a flash of light and angels and things. There wasn't anything at all. I just sat there in the dingy church. But it was strange, because when I got up to go I did feel a little better. When I got home Dad was there, and he was looking really, really shattered and he was crying. I've never seen him cry before. It made me feel terrible. So I put my arms around him and gave him a big hug. And then he told me that Linda had lost the baby. I know I didn't want that baby around, but I didn't want everything to end up like this. It was an awful thing to happen. And I thought about all the things she'd bought, and how happy she was about the baby and it was really awful. Dad says he doesn't think Linda will ever get over this because she wanted that baby so much.

September 17th

Linda is back home now. They say they won't need to operate, but she will have to be on medication for the rest of her life. She looks really ill and has to rest a lot. I don't know what to say to her. I feel really bad about the baby, and I will do my best not to irritate her or get in her face for a while. I feel so sorry for her. It's sad.

September 25th
Things are still difficult. Linda seems to be okay, but I keep hearing her cry in her room. Dad's going nuts with worry about it all. Anyway, I'm trying to help. I'm not playing music loud and I haven't done anything to make her freak out. But it's really hard because she's so down on me now. I don't know if I'm right, but I think she kind of blames me for still being alive when her daughter's dead. I keep out of the house as much as I can. Jazz and me go out a lot and I really wish we could get an apartment together after my birthday. It's not easy living here.

From The Desk of Linda Richmond

September 27th

Dear Paula,

Thanks for the flowers and all the encouraging letters and phone calls. I feel so dreadful just now. Everything seems like too much effort. I know that Marty is doing her best, but just the sight of her seems to irritate me at the moment. All I can think of is that I've lost my chance to have a daughter now. It breaks my heart. And apart from that I have to be on medication for the rest of my life. I feel as if I am too young to have to put up with that. Kevin is being fantastic and really caring. But I don't seem able to feel much about anything. I wonder if he was secretly relieved that I lost the baby. He says he isn't but a bit of me just has to wonder.

The worst of it all is that the doctor says there is very little chance of my conceiving again. It's my worst nightmare, I think. Marty doesn't know that I am unlikely to have another child, but I'm sure she will be happy about it anyway. That's not fair—forget I wrote that. She really has got a softer side, and was as shocked as any of us when I had the heart attack and lost the baby. It's just that fundamentally I don't think anything will ever change between us.

To add to my despair, Melanie is coming over from Mexico City next week. Apparently she's won a plane ticket in a competition, and is flying over for a week. She won't stay with us, of course. She'll be staying with Wedgie, but I really do dread it. Kevin says I shouldn't get so worked up about things and that everything is okay. He says that Mel has moved on with her life and is perfectly happy with her new husband. But a bit of me feels really insecure about her coming. And how will it affect Marty? We are still on eggshells with each other, but at least it is a sort of armed neutrality. What happens if Mel comes along and upsets all that? I don't think I can face it.

All the best,

Linda

September 28th

Hurray! Mom's coming here next week. She won a ticket in a competition. Juan's taking time off work to look after Xavier and she's flying over just for one week. I can't believe it! It will be so great to have her around, especially after all the things that have been happening here. I don't think Linda's too pleased. But remember Marty you're going to try not to be bitchy about your stepmom anymore. I must keep remembering that she's having a very bad time. I just wish she wouldn't be so difficult all the time. Jazz says I have to be as understanding as possible. He doesn't live here or he wouldn't say that. I just left a bit of a mess in the bathroom yesterday and she went completely nuts! She was like a deranged woman. She said I never thought of anybody but myself and that she was sick of it. I told Jazz about it, and he said I had to try and think calm, karmically good thoughts—whatever they are. I know he was talking about karma, but really, is karmically even a word? I didn't say anything. Jazz was just being sweet.

Marty's Diary

October 2nd

I can't believe Mom's here. She looks so tanned and happy and is full of energy. She bought some nice presents for us all, including a really great Aztec necklace for Linda. But Linda hardly looked at it. It's really awkward when we're all together, although Mom tries to keep the conversation going. She says she's going to take me to town tomorrow for a break. I can't wait!

October 3rd

Mom and I had a great time in town. We went and tried on lots of clothes in Sundays Boutique and she met Rafaella, the owner, who's going to give me a part-time job there next year. Then we went to have lunch in a fancy Italian place. I asked Mom if she'd won the lottery because it was one of those places where they don't put the prices on the menu, but she just laughed. She said couldn't she treat her only daughter if she wanted to? We talked about what had happened to Linda. Mom said she is feeling really sad. Mom knows about miscarrying because she lost a baby before she had me. She said that people sometimes feel angry as well when it happens, and that I had to be understanding with Linda for the moment. I told her it was very hard because she was so difficult. Then I told her about Jazz and what he said. She said she would like to meet him and so we went to his house on the way home. I think she thought he was okay. Everybody likes Jazz. He's so easy with everyone. After we'd left him I could see Mom was dying to ask if we were having sex, but she couldn't get the words out. So I saved her the trouble and told her we were, and that I was on the pill (after our scare, which I didn't tell her about!). She said that was okay.

When we got back home Linda made another scene about nothing very much. It was embarrassing. Mom was great. She pretended not to notice what was going on. She gave me a hug and went off back to Auntie Wedgie's. We're going round there tomorrow night for dinner. I can't wait—NOT! It's bound to be tense.

Marty's Diary

October 4th

That has to be the most horrible dinner I was ever at. Auntie Wedgie talked non-stop because I think she was trying to pretend that everything was wonderful. After my mom's fine words about being understanding with Linda, she and my stepmom ended up locking horns about a few things. Dad just looked as if he would rather be somewhere else, and Uncle Bob chewed his dinner and looked bored. It was terrible. And then Mom had to make it a zillion times worse. She said, "I am sorry for your loss, Linda, but I don't think you should make life difficult for Marty and Kevin." Well that did it! It turned into a shouting match with Auntie Wedgie trying to ask people if they wanted apple crumble to calm them down. Anyway, in the end nobody was talking to anybody else and we all went home. I swear to God I'm never getting married, or having babies. This whole family thing is a major disaster.

October 10th

Things are better here today. I never thought I'd say this, but since Mom's gone back to

Mexico things are easier. The trouble is that she and Linda don't like each other and that's that. Jazz says I am getting very mature in my outlook about my crazy family. Maybe it's just that I am beginning to feel less concerned about things now. I am definitely going to go to nursing school. At least Linda has done one thing for me. In the last few days she's been encouraging Dad to be more positive about that idea. He's not happy but said he wouldn't stop me from applying.

October 19th
This is fantastic! Linda said she would go with me to City College to ask them about AA courses. I've got enough credits to graduate. Hurray! I'm going to be a nurse and soothe fevered brows. Linda actually laughed when I told her that. Maybe there is actually a sense of humor lurking inside my stepmom after all.

From The Desk of Linda Richmond

October 24th

Dear Paula,

How are you? It seems to me that all our contact recently has been about me. Me and my aches and pains and sadnesses. I think I'm rather selfish and should have been asking much more about how you're doing.

Strangely enough, since I got back from the hospital things between Marty and me aren't so bad. It didn't start off spectacularly well because I was feeling so upset and angry about the baby and the heart attack and everything. I am afraid I was quite snappy with her and Kevin and with Mel when she turned up from Mexico. But it was difficult, and somehow that woman just gets on my nerves. She seems so smug about what she's got. And I feel she'd like to rub my nose in it. In fact, we almost came to blows at one point when we were having a meal with Wedgie. Poor old Wedgie was sitting in the middle *trying to keep the peace and rambling on about apple crumble! It was a serious disaster.*

But things are calming down now. Marty is desperate to go to nursing school. Ever since I have been on the scene this has been a dream of hers, and I don't really understand why Kevin is so down on the idea. He really wants her to get a business degree which I think is quite unsuitable for her and would bore her. Anyway, I felt it was time I tried to intervene a bit on her behalf. Between us we managed to persuade Kevin to let her make enquiries at City College. They were happy about her interest and gave her an application. Perhaps now things will settle more.

All the best,

Linda

October 28th

Things are a bit quiet here just now. It's just studying and then my part-time job at Sundays Boutique. I met Zoe there and she's really great. She's the same age as me and we've become good friends. I told her all about the audition for the X Factor and she says I should try and enter other talent shows because I've got a good voice. I don't know if I will though. Anyway we have a great time at Sundays because Rafaella lets us try on the stock when it's slow. Not that I can afford to buy anything there at $140 for a belt! Things at home are quieter as well. Linda seems to have got over her loss now. She's gone a bit weird though and is way into homoeopathy and reiki healing and all that. She says that she's got to get in touch with her inner self whatever that means. And she's been reading a lot of self-awareness books. Anyway, whatever's right for her. At least she seems less stressed and that's good. She told me one good thing though, about Rescue Remedy, which are these fabulous drops that you can take if you're stressed. You're only supposed to have a few but I reckon I might take the whole bottle when I have to take my exams. I am finding something out now about Linda. If I don't try and think of her as my stepmother, but just another person, I feel better about her. I don't know if that is the right way to feel, but there it is.

November 5th

Halloween was fun and Jazz and me had a good time down at Dean's house. Linda's gone crazy. She's really lost it. It's official. She's got mixed up with all these weird types, and now she's joined a group set up for stepparents and their stepchildren. It's called A Step Forward and she's asked me if I will come with her to a meeting next Thursday. She says we can explore our inner selves and find the real meaning of things, and what it means to be stepparents and stepchildren. Her friend Portia says we will be able to find each other in the circle of light which sounds wacko to me. I asked Dad what he thought about it, and he just shrugged his shoulders. I think he doesn't really care as long as Linda is enjoying herself a bit more. So next Thursday (unless I want Linda never to speak to me again) I have to go to the community center down the road and talk about my inner self.

From The Desk of Linda Richmond

November 5th

Dear Paula,

I am feeling much better and so much more enlightened. I've got my friend Margaret Roberts coming to do Feng Shui in the house and I'm sure that will help too. I think all the energies in the house are flowing the wrong way. And in the meantime, guess what? Through my friends at the Reiki Center, I've found a fabulous new friend (Portia) who is also (yes, you've guessed) a stepmom. It was such a relief to talk to somebody who knows about these things. Anyway, she's invited me and Marty to a group she attends called A Step Forward. It's a group set up by men and women in the same position as us. Apparently it is wonderful. She says we get to explore the parameters of the new relationship and how it works. I am all for that. Anything to help.

All the best,

Linda

From The Desk of Linda Richmond

November 8th

Dear Paula,

The A Step Forward evening was a huge success! Marty was quiet but I think she enjoyed herself. Portia was wonderful and introduced me to lots of the other stepmoms. May Ling who runs the organization makes everything seem easy. Her relationship with her own stepdaughter is clearly working. The daughter never left her side all evening. And there were other people there who had lots of useful tips and hints for improving communication. May Ling organizes a circle of friendship and we all hold hands. Then when somebody feels compelled to say something, they do. All kinds of things are revealed. Some of it was touching, some of it was funny, but the main thing was that I didn't feel so much alone. I think for that reason alone A Step Forward has to be a good thing. Hopefully I can get Marty to go again. They have these sessions twice a month in *the community center. Admittedly it's a bit chilly in there and not quite conducive to this sort of thing, but it's better to have it there than never to have it at all.*

All the best,

Linda

November 8th

Oh heavens! A Step Forward—what are they like? This woman May Ling got us all to stand in a circle of friendship and hold hands. I felt like an idiot. Then she went on about how it was called A Step Forward because stepparent/children relationships can only go one step at a time. She said that her own stepdaughter Luce was a wonderful example of how this relationship can work. Funny, I thought that Luce looked totally pathetic. She never said a word all evening. I guess she's about my age, but May Ling had dressed her in some sort of long skirt with a dipping hem and a funny top. She looked way weird. Hmm, I thought, this wonderful relationship is working for you, but is it working for her? Linda thought it was absolutely wonderful and wants me to go next week. I suppose I'll have to, just to keep her happy. But they shouldn't expect me to say anything. I noticed this time that the stepparents had a lot to say, but the teenagers said nothing much. Except for one boy who was called Larry. I guess he was about fifteen and he was really radical. His stepmom was a skinny frightened-looking woman. Anyway, I can think of better things to do on a Thursday evening.

From The Desk of Linda Richmond

November 15th

Dear Paula,

We had another marvelous session at A Step Forward. There were one or two awkward moments, one of them unfortunately due to Marty. But it's so liberating to talk to other people who are in the same position as me, and May Ling is such an example to us all. I suggested to Marty that we invite her and Luce over some time. I said maybe we could have a girls' night in or something. Marty muttered something which may or may not have been agreement. But I think it might be nice for her to spend some time with Luce. After all they are in the same situation. Mind you, May Ling really does seem to have got this whole stepparenting angst completely worked out. Luce seems absolutely devoted to her. You know May Ling's always so ready to give me helpful advice and tips on how to proceed. And she told me not to be too upset about what

Marty had said. She said it was just underlying resentment which had not yet been resolved.

All the best,

Linda

November 15th

Well if my crazy bizzaro stepma thinks I am going anywhere near that nutty A Step Forward again, she's wacked. It was all so humiliating. It started off all right with everyone treading carefully around each other. The stepparents spoke loads more than the stepchildren again. In fact, you couldn't shut them up. It was like they were on a roll. But then one of the teenagers spoke. It was my friend Larry again. And by the time he'd finished speaking there was a deafening silence. But I thought he made sense. He said that all this artificial bonding was pointless. He said it was a waste of time and completely false. You could have heard a pin drop. Nobody said anything at all for a few moments. And then I just couldn't sit there any longer. So I stood up and said I agreed with him. I saw May Ling and Linda raise their eyebrows at each other and that made me mad. So I said that it was ridiculous to expect stepchildren and stepparents to get along. Then May Ling asked me what I thought of Linda. She said, in that syrupy way she has, "Can you share with the group your feelings about

Linda, Marty?" And something snapped in me. I said I wished that people would stop asking me that. Because the truth is I don't feel anything about Linda at all. And there was another silence. Nobody spoke, and Linda looked tragic. Why the hell did they have to ask if they didn't want the answer? So anyway it was all really uncomfortable until somebody made a joke to release the tension.

When I was going out, Larry gave me his mobile number and said I should keep in touch. I might. Larry's okay. At least he speaks honestly. And he doesn't do all the bullshit about everybody loving everybody and circles of light and crap.

November 18th
Linda's not really speaking to me. We haven't talked about what happened the other day. I didn't want to hurt her, but I had to be honest. I have a mom and I don't want another one. And Linda was nothing to me until she married my dad. So why should I suddenly have to be her very best friend

and loving relation? It doesn't make sense. And why everybody's on my case about this I don't know. Linda was a stranger. She's still a stranger. So it's crazy to expect me to see her as an extra mom.

December 2nd

Hurray! Juan's coming to visit! He's coming over here on business. Something to do with gallery exhibits. I wanted him to stay with us. But he said it would be better if he was a bit closer to the gallery he was visiting. I just don't think he wants to stay with Dad and Linda. He'll be here in four days. I can't wait!

December 7th

I can't believe it! Juan has managed to work his special magic on Linda. When he arrived she was as prickly as a cactus and I wondered how he would manage. But he just smiled at her and said her lemon cake was the best cake he's ever tasted and she was putty in his hands! And when she got a bit standoffish when he was talking about

Mom, he didn't take any notice at all. He just went on chatting. I wonder if that's the way to cope with awkward situations like that, just fill in the silence. But Dad was the funniest. I could see he had mixed feelings about Juan. After all, he's got Dad's ex. He was a bit frosty as well, but Juan soon had him eating out of the palm of his hand. Juan said he was going to treat us all to a large and tasty meal at Giovinazzo's tomorrow night. But Linda and Dad said they couldn't make it so me and Juan are going together. He said I could bring a friend along if I wanted, but Jazz is busy that night.

December 9th
We had a great meal at Giovinazzo's. We had all sorts of things including a pasta called "little ears" which is a speciality of southern Italy, especially Puglia. And we talked about anything and everything. He filled me in on what Mom was doing and all about Xavier and how he's getting to be a toddler. Then there was a bit of an awkward silence, as if he was wondering how to bring up the next thing. But I saved him the bother

because I'd already guessed. "It's Mom," I said. "She's pregnant." He could see I wasn't upset about it, and in fact quite pleased. Maybe it means I'm growing up. But I don't feel so left out about this one, even if it is a girl. He never talked at all about Dad and Linda during the meal. Then right at the end he said, "Marty, how are things going with you and Linda now?" I like Juan. He's direct. He doesn't beat around the bush. So I shrugged my shoulders and said they weren't good or bad particularly. Things are just as they were and that was that. And he said that was a really mature attitude. Then I told him all about A Step Forward and he laughed. But he said that he could understand why people wanted to try to improve step-relationships. Also he said that he could understand why I feel as I do, and that it isn't my fault if I can't feel different. It's ridiculous—he's not even my relative and yet I can almost speak to him more easily than I can my dad.

From The Desk of Linda Richmond

December 10th

Dear Paula,

Well I am still continuing to go to A Step Forward although Marty refuses to come with me. She just gets obstructive and says she's not going to go and watch people talking a lot of artificial crap, and anyway it's boring. Boring indeed! But there we are—I suppose that's teenagers. Personally, I find May Ling an absolute inspiration. Nothing seems to get her down.

Juan has come over from Mexico City. I wasn't sure what I would make of him, but it turns out he's absolutely charming. He's easy company and laughs a lot, and is very knowledgeable about many things. I'm glad to have met him as I was feeling a bit tentative about it. He told us that Mel is pregnant again. I wonder how this will affect Marty. I hope she doesn't feel more pushed out because of the impending new arrival. Anyway, Juan seems to make her *feel quite secure and happy and they went out for a meal together from which she came back quite happy and relaxed. He certainly seems a good influence on her generally.*

All the best,

Linda

December 12th

Juan went back today and I felt quite sad. Anyway, he's taking a present from me for Mom and Xavier. I got Xavier a pull-along car which Juan says he will like because he's nuts about cars, and a blue top for my mom. Just before he went and when we were on our own he said that he never gave advice unless he was asked, but there was one thing he wanted to say. He said that it's much easier to get along with people when we accept them just as they are. Just as I find it hard to accept Linda as she is, she probably finds it hard to accept me as I am too. He said people are basically the same. They are all frightened and lonely and angry and difficult, and kind and loving and thoughtful and everything else. And so all we need is a bit of understanding. I WILL TRY HARDER.

December 26th

Well, I tried and it didn't work! She drives me nuts and that's that. You know everybody is supposed to reach out to each other over Christmas and all that, following the example set by Jesus? I wonder how he'd have coped with a stepmom when he was a teenager. I bet he wouldn't have found it straightforward at all. She's so in my face. And she still manages to come between me and my dad. I've tried to be mature about it. But the truth is that I really resent her. He's my dad and I would like to have more time by myself with him. But she doesn't seem to realize that. She thinks they are glued together in a sort of package. And so if he takes me anywhere she tags along as well. I think even Wedgie noticed and tried to suggest he spend a bit of time just with me. But Dad seems to be totally under Linda's thumb since her heart attack. He will never do anything to upset her. Also I think that he's feeling guilty about the baby and everything. I don't think in his heart he was totally committed to the idea of another baby at his age. Anyway, Christmas was horrible. It gets more horrible each year. Next year I'm going to try and be with Mom and Juan. I hate it so much. Everybody starts off trying to be nice and it always ends up in nasty little arguments.

January 1st

A new year. I've made a resolution. I'm not going to let Linda get to me. I'm going to be more detached about everything. For starters, I'm going to take up Wedgie's suggestion that I go and stay with her for a bit. Uncle Bob is there less and less. Everybody knows the marriage is over, so I think Auntie Wedgie's quite lonely. I think it will be easier not to be with Dad and Linda, day in and day out. I'm going next week. I can't wait.

From The Desk of Linda Richmond

January 1st

Dear Paula,

Well here we are at the start of another year. I feel a bit down actually. I've tried so hard with Marty and now she's announced that she's going to stay with Wedgie for a bit. I got a bit upset after she told us the news because I've tried so hard to bond with her. And Kevin wasn't much help either. He said that he thought perhaps I was trying too hard. He said it might have been better if I'd just let her come to things in her own way. I wanted to retort that that wouldn't be in my lifetime but I bit my tongue. So she's going next week. Maybe it's for the best. Perhaps Kevin and I can have some quality time together without any interruptions. The baby issue still hangs between us. It would be unlikely that I could conceive again anyway, but I do feel sad that Kevin won't even talk about it, or about the baby I lost. Anyway, as you say, *it's the start of a new year and so I must make the most of it. Who knows what fate has in store for us?*

With best wishes,

Linda

January 20th

I should have moved in with Wedgie before. She says I must stop calling her auntie now as it makes her feel old. We've always got along and it's great. Bob used my arrival to announce that he was leaving altogether. And Wedgie said good riddance to bad rubbish. He's gone to live with his trashy woman (a bottle blonde with bad teeth) who lives on Devon Road. And she's welcome to him. Wedgie seems much happier without him. She's doing really well at her job now, and Mr. Patel has opened another dry cleaners which she's managing as well. So more money. She looks good, and I can't believe she's the same aunt who was crying at the kitchen table in a ratty old bathrobe. I'm staying in the room where I used to sleep when I came over to visit when I was little. It's just the same, and I like that. There's a white bed and a white cupboard and a big poster of a flower painting. The curtains and bedspread are blue and it's a cool place to be. I feel so happy here. Nobody nags me and Wedgie never shouts about the mess. Maybe she doesn't notice it either. I miss my dad of course, and I miss Linda's cooking. Wedgie's a terrible cook! But that's all. And of course Spotty the dog is here, and I've always liked him a lot.

January 29th

I've been thinking about things recently. Wedgie said it might be good sometime to sort out in my mind what I really feel about Linda and all that. She said write it all down. And so here goes diary! I resent Linda for taking my dad away from me. I don't think I'll ever get over that. And I resent Dad for messing up and letting Mom go like that. It seems to me that I lost both parents at the same time. I kind of understand about Mom though, and I find it very easy to be fond of Juan. He doesn't judge me—he seems to accept me. And he's really straight and honest about things. He doesn't beat around the bush like Linda. I am getting used to the idea of Mom's new family now as well. But what's happened with Dad and Linda is different. I think Dad let me down by marrying her. He must have known I would find it hard. I know it's childish but I didn't want to share him with her. And I don't really like Linda much either. If she had been the sort of person I could have grown fond of or if she wasn't my stepmother it might have been different. But she isn't. I don't think the same way as her, I don't understand her, and I don't like the things she stands for. And you know what, diary? I think that's okay. Where is it written in the rule book that I, Marty, have to bond with and love my stepmom? Everybody's different, and it's ridiculous to say that we will all be able to get along. So that's the truth as I see it.

From The Desk of Linda Richmond

January 30th

Dear Paula,

How are you? Things are quite quiet here, and in some ways peaceful. Marty is now staying with Wedgie, and I doubt if she'll ever come back here. It won't be long until she starts nursing school anyway. She's looking forward to that. I know that Kevin is disappointed she's left home. I think he also feels a bit guilty. Marty hinted before she left that she felt he'd let her down a bit by neglecting her since he married me. He feels very sad about that, but I think he can see that there is only a limited amount of fence-mending he can do at present. But her going has given us a chance to sort out our relationship. The sadness he feels about Marty does affect our relationship. In some ways he blames me for the situation. I think he was unrealistic from the start about all this. He must have realized that it would be difficult for her suddenly to acquire a surrogate mom at her age. And because I

was unsure of myself, I suspect I made the situation a lot worse.

If I had been more confident, things might have been better. Marty doesn't know me any more than I know her, and that's a tragedy. At the end of the day, the situation is what it is, and I can't see it ever really changing. When you wrote before you asked if I was fond of her. And the odd thing is that some of the time I am. The rest of the time she drives me nuts! But I don't think she feels the same way about me. Anyway, I've promised myself one thing. I'm going to write to her and tell her what I think of everything. At least then I will have communicated what I really want to tell her. A bit of me is sad that there was a potential for a relationship which will never now be realized. It started off wrong and got worse, and none of us knew how to correct it, or how to change it for the better. I believe that to be the truth. And that's what I'm going to tell her. And of course, I have that other news to share with her.

With best wishes,

Linda

February 6th

This is going to be my last diary entry for the time being. I have too much to do now to write in it—I want to graduate, and Jazz and I want to start a band with his friend Zain in our spare time. He's asked me to try and think up a name for it. Jazz has written some great songs.

I had a letter from Linda a few days ago. It was kind of sad really. She said she was sorry if she had made a mess of being a stepmom, but she'd had no experience at being a mom of any kind, let alone a stepmom. She said we started on the wrong foot and that was a shame. And I agree with her. One hundred per cent. The trouble is that I can't change how I feel. She changed my relationship with my dad and it will never be the same, and I can't accept that really easily. I can't be her friend because we aren't alike, not like me and Wedgie for example, and she can't be my stepmom because I have a mom already. The truth is that at the end of the day there is no room in my life for her. Not in a way which means anything. I think the only thing I can do is accept that. And it will make life much easier for me if she can as well. I promise myself one thing though. When I get married it's for keeps. I don't want any child of mine to have a stepparent. Maybe that sounds harsh but that's how I feel. But the good thing about all this I think, and Jazz agrees with me, is all this unhappiness has made me a bit more independent. And I don't think that's a bad thing.

The other thing that Linda wrote was that she is pregnant again. I could see from the way she wrote she was a bit anxious about telling me. So she put it right at the end of the letter. She said she hoped very much that I would be able to be part of the baby's life. And after thinking about it for a bit, I really think I can. After all, this baby is my blood and that counts for something. I know that I felt a bit jealous of Xavier to begin with, but I am getting quite fond of him now. Especially now he's stopped pooing and peeing all the time.

I've been talking to Wedgie. She was quite pleased for Linda about the baby.

And she says she thinks the baby might help everyone to get some perspective on everything. Wedgie says that babies are healing. We'll see. Let's hope for the best. After all, that's all any of us can do.